The Almond Orchard

Laura Jane Coats

Macmillan Publishing Company
New York

Collier Macmillan Canada
Toronto

Maxwell Macmillan International Publishing Group
New York   Oxford   Singapore   Sydney

For their assistance in reviewing the manuscript, the author would like to thank Warren Micke, Extension Pomologist, University of California at Davis; Dan Campbell, editor of *Almond Facts*; and Embry Fantozzi, caretaker of the orchard described in the book.

Macmillan Publishing Company
866 Third Avenue, New York, NY 10022

Collier Macmillan Canada, Inc.
1200 Eglinton Avenue East, Suite 200
Don Mills, Ontario M3C 3N1

First edition
Printed in Hong Kong

10   9   8   7   6   5   4   3   2   1

The text of this book is set in 13 point Palatino.
The illustrations are rendered in pencil and watercolor.

Library of Congress Cataloging-in-Publication Data
Coats, Laura Jane.
The almond orchard / Laura Jane Coats.—1st ed.   p.   cm.
Summary: A woman remembers helping her family tend their almond orchard through the seasons as she was growing up and contemplates the changes that technology has brought to the process.
ISBN 0-02-719041-2
[1. Orchards—Fiction. 2. Almond—Fiction. 3. Seasons—Fiction.]
I. Title.
PZ7.C6293AL 1991 [E]—dc20 90-38009 CIP AC

To my grandmother,

Rosemary Ballard Redhair

When I was a little girl, my family lived in a house in the middle of an open valley. Behind the house was an almond orchard, which my father had planted. My father ran the general store in our town, but growing almonds was the work he loved best.

All through my childhood, I watched the trees grow and change with the seasons. In early summer, young almonds covered the branches. As the almonds grew, each formed its own shell, protected on the outside by a velvety green hull. Papa worked hard to keep the orchard clear of weeds. Toward the end of summer, he smoothed the ground to prepare for harvest.

Gradually the hulls turned golden brown and split open to reveal the almond shells. Late in summer, the ripe almonds began to drop from the branches. Papa hired someone to mind the store, and over the next six weeks he harvested almonds.

Many of the young men in our area took part in the harvest. Papa paid them a dollar a day to knock almonds. The men spread canvas tarps on the ground. Then they hit the trees with rubber mallets and shook the branches with long poles to knock the almonds onto the tarps. I helped by picking up the almonds that fell at the edges.

Once the almonds were down, the men dragged the tarps to one
side and emptied them onto a long, flat sled. Each time they filled
the sled, a horse pulled it to a work shed at the edge of the orchard.
There, Mama and my sisters removed the hulls, leaving the almonds
in their shells.

Since the shells were damp and the moisture could spoil the nuts, Papa laid the almonds in the sun to dry. To speed the drying, he turned them with a rake every morning and afternoon. A few days later, he shoveled the dried almonds into burlap sacks. My brother sewed the sacks shut and helped load them onto a wagon.

At last the almonds were ready. Papa hitched the horses to the wagon, piled high with the heavy sacks. My brother and I rode along as he drove the wagon to the train station. Later we watched the train chug off to the city with our almonds.

Papa sold the crop to a man in the city who bought almonds from many growers. The selling price changed from year to year, but Papa usually got about five cents a pound for the almonds. Our eight-acre orchard produced four thousand pounds in an average year.

The city man who bought our almonds sent them to storekeepers

in different parts of the country. Customers scooped the almonds

from a burlap sack, and the storekeeper weighed them, charging

by the pound.

In the almond orchard, new buds already had formed on the branches, although they would not begin to grow for many weeks. The weather cooled, and soon the leaves changed color and fell to the ground. It was time to prune the trees.

In the early hours before his store opened, Papa worked in the orchard. He removed a few branches from each tree so that when summer came more sunlight would reach the almonds. My brother gathered the fallen branches into piles to be hauled away and burned.

Toward the end of autumn, Papa lined the orchard with smudge pots, which he had filled with fuel oil. In the cold months ahead, he would light the smudge pots. Their smoky fires would protect the trees from frost.

Soon the winter rains came, soaking the orchard floor. Some years we had a drought, and Papa worried that the crop would be poor. But with normal rainfall, the soil absorbed enough water to nourish the trees throughout the coming summer.

The weeks passed, and as spring drew near the days became slightly warmer. We saw the tips of flower petals emerging from the tiny buds.

Here and there, the buds began to open. Then one morning I woke to find the orchard white with blossoms. Their sweet smell filled the air.

Bees moved busily from one flower to another, gathering nectar and pollen. At the same time, they pollinated the trees. This ensured that the inside of each flower would grow to become a soft nutlet.

Rain or freezing temperatures would ruin the flowers, so we hoped for dry weather during blossom time. And if frost seemed

likely, Papa lit the smudge pots.

The blossoms soon faded, and the delicate petals floated to the ground. Leaves sprouted and the nutlets started to grow, beginning a new cycle of seasons.

But even in spring, the nights were sometimes cold, and frost would harm the soft nutlets. Papa kept the smudge pots in the orchard until late spring, when the nutlets had hardened into young almonds.

Over the years, I saw many springtimes come and go. And although I moved away when I grew up, I always thought of the house in the valley as home. When Papa was very old, he gave part of the almond orchard to me. By that time he had planted over seventy acres of trees.

I hired a caretaker to handle the seasonal chores and manage the harvest. He put in a well and an electric pump to bring more water to the orchard. If a tree became too old to produce a good yield, he cut it down, dug out the stump, and helped me plant a seedling.

Today, at blossom time, he rents hives from a beekeeper to make certain that pollination occurs. And instead of lighting smudge pots, he turns on wind machines. These keep the air moving so that frost cannot form on the trees.

Many other changes have come about since Papa first planted
the orchard. Tractors and trailers have replaced horses and wagons.
During harvest, a mechanical shaker knocks the almonds. It grips
each tree trunk and vibrates, bringing a shower of almonds to the
ground. Spinning brushes clear the way so that the wheels of the

shaker do not crush the nuts.

Then a mechanical sweeper pushes the almonds into rows. A pickup machine follows, blowing out leaves and dirt as it scoops the almonds into a trailer bin. Finally, a mechanical huller removes the hulls, which are saved and fed to livestock.

A conveyer belt transfers the almonds to bins on the back of a
truck. Then a driver delivers the crop to an almond processing plant.
He turns a crank, opening a panel beneath each bin. The almonds
fall through a funnel, past a grate, and into an underground chamber.

Samples are checked for quality. Then the almonds are stored

in silos, where cool temperatures keep them from spoiling. Later machines remove the almond shells, gently cracking them without damaging the nuts. The shells are burned, creating electricity to power the processing plant.

Inside the plant, almonds from many orchards are slivered, sliced, chopped, diced, blanched, roasted, salted, toasted, seasoned, and ground into powder and paste. They are packaged in bags, jars, cans, and boxes, then labeled and shipped all over the world.

Many of the almonds are sent to companies that make ice cream,

candies, and cookies. Others go to restaurants, where chefs prepare trout amandine and almond tarts and soufflés.

Researchers have perfected age-old methods of making almond oil, almond butter, and almond soaps and lotions. And they continue to develop ideas for new almond products.

But not everything has changed. I worry about the crop, just as Papa did, when the weather is too cold or too dry. Although I can no longer help with the work, I still make sure that the trees are well cared for. And I always go home when the almond orchard is in bloom.